for
with much
love
and lots of
kisses
♡ Tonnie

FOR

D.B.D.

Copyright © 1973 by Tomie de Paola

Printed in the United States of America • J

Prentice-Hall International, Inc., London
Prentice-Hall of Australia, Pty. Ltd., North Sydney
Prentice-Hall of Canada, Ltd., Toronto
Prentice-Hall of India Private Ltd., New Delhi
Prentice-Hall of Japan, Inc., Tokyo

Library of Congress Cataloging in Publication Data

De Paola, Thomas Anthony.
Andy: that's my name.

SUMMARY: Andy's friends construct different words
from his name: "an" words, "and" words, and "andy"
words.
I. Title.
PZ7.D439An   [E]   73-4593
ISBN 0-13-036731-1

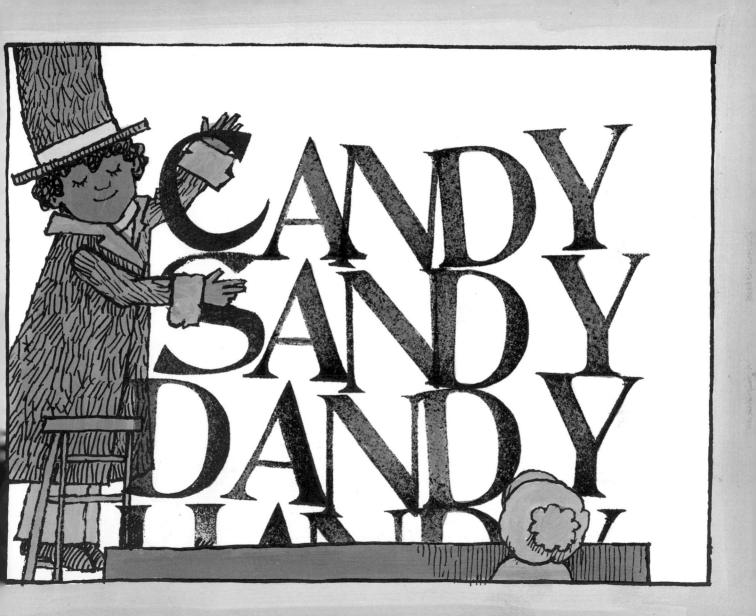